NEW HAVEN PUBLIC LIBRARY
3 5000 09417 4991
W9-ALL-513
DATE DUE
OCT 0 2 2007
APR 0 5 2016
OCT 2 5 2007
JAN 2 0 2009
DEC 0 4 2007
JAN 0 7 2010
FEB 1 1 2008
APR 1 5 2008
FEB 0 6 2010
MAY 1 6 2008
JUL 2 2 2010
JUL 0 1 2008
NOV 1 3 2010
AUG 2 2 2008
NOV 2 0 2008
FEB 2 6 2011
JUN 1 3 2013
DEC 0 4 2008
DEC 1 9 2011
GAYLORD
PRINTED IN U.S.A.
6
7

For Lorcan and Augusta
Born 6th July 2005 ♡♡

A big thank-you to everyone at Walker Books, especially David and Audrey

First U.S. edition 2007

Library of Congress Cataloging-in-Publication Data is available.

Library of Congress Catalog Card Number 2005053641

ISBN 978-0-7636-2986-1

10 9 8 7 6 5 4 3 2 1

Printed in Singapore

This book was typeset in LNSpanyolSemiBold.
The illustrations were done in pen and gouache.

Candlewick Press
2067 Massachusetts Avenue
Cambridge, Massachusetts 02140

www.candlewick.com

# Little Neighbors on Sunnyside Street

Jessica Spanyol

CANDLEWICK PRESS
CAMBRIDGE, MASSACHUSETTS

# Welcome to Sunnyside Street.

Let's meet some of the *Little Neighbors* who live on Sunnyside Street. They have lots of fun things to do today.

**Ian** and his little sister, *Baby Jade*, live at number 4. **Ian** really likes playing with *Baby Jade*, and he is very good at it.

Kelly lives at number 5. It is a pretty house, but sometimes it gets a little messy.

The Bugs live at number 6. It is a funny little house with lots and lots of garages.

Philip lives at number 7. Today he is busy collecting cardboard boxes.

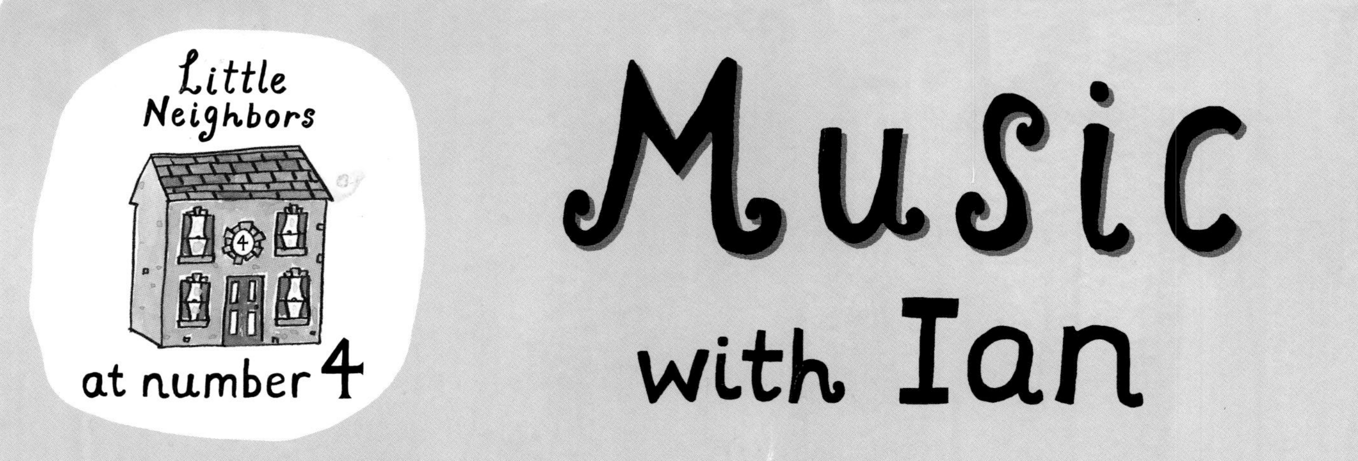


# Music with Ian

**Ian** really likes music, and he is very good at it. Here he is getting out his instruments: a xylophone, a flute, and a drum. **Ian's** little sister, *Baby Jade*, loves the way **Ian** plays her favorite song.

"Twinkle, twinkle,
little star,
How I wonder
what you are.

Up above the world
so high,
Like a diamond
in the sky...."

BOOM!
BOOM!
BOOM!
"Good drumming, Ian!"

# Driving with the Bugs

All the Bugs are out driving in the backyard.
All the Bugs like driving.

Tate likes driving his vintage car.

Keith likes driving his sizzling Firebug.

The Triplets like driving their convertible.

Mr. Thornton-Jones likes giving his friends a ride in his Beetle.

Jo-Jo likes driving her van. She painted the flowers herself.

*Stacie* likes driving her classy car.

**Bob** likes driving his bubble car.

Giorgio likes driving his racing car.

Pauline and the girls like driving their Jeep.

Clemence likes driving his tiny yellow car.

And most of all, they love to . . .

bump and bash!
Beeeeep!
"Whee! Go, Jo-Jo, go!"
Beep! Beep!
"Gotcha, Tate!"
I ♥ DriVing
Go Jo-Jo go
"Again, again!"
"Again, again!"
"Look at us!"
"Oops! My glasses!"
"Whee! I'm flying!"
3
1, 2, 3, go!
Beetle
Bump!
Bump!

Bash!
"Come on, Bob!"
Bump!
Beep! Beep! Beep!
"Come on, Giorgio!"
Classy
Brumm!
Brumm!
"Off I go."
Bubble
"Whee!"
"Yippee! again, again!"
"OK, girls. Let's get Keith!"
Hoot!
Jeep
Firebug
"WOW! This is fun!"
Hoot!
Hoot!
Bash!

# Making Things with Philip

Philip likes making things.

Today he needs:

1 cardboard box
1 teddy bear
1 pair of scissors
1 jar of paint
1 brush

tape / pens / pencils

"Cut one big hole in the box and paint some stars like this," says Philip.

"Then put the box over your head and . . .
zoom, zoom, zoom,
we're going to the moon.
5, 4, 3, 2, 1 . . .
BLAST OFF!"

# Messy Play with Kelly

Kelly is playing in her room. She really likes making a big mess. Here comes Mom, who wants to help Kelly clean up.

“Books here, darling,” says Mom.

“Let’s hang up some clothes. Good girl, Kelly, dear.

“And all the toys in the box.

“That’s nice and neat. Now, I’ll be back in a minute. . . .”

"Oh, Kelly, dear!"

# Reading

Philip likes reading his songbook.

"Teddy bear, teddy bear,
in your box.
Teddy bear, teddy bear,
tucked in tight.
Teddy bear, teddy bear,
turn out the light.
Teddy bear, teddy bear,
say
**good night!**"

The Bugs like reading books about driving.

"All aboard the bug train! Here we go!

Clickety clack, Clickety clack, Clickety clack."

Kelly likes reading
lots of books.

Oops!
Oops!
Oops!
Oops!
Oops!
Oops!
Oops!
Oops!

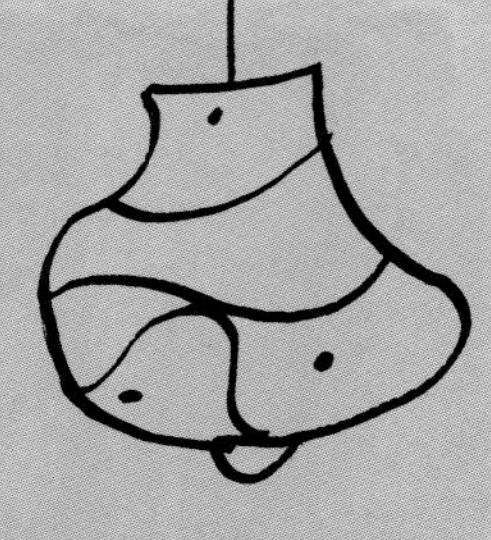

**Ian** likes reading,
and he is very good at it.
**Ian's** little sister, *Baby Jade*,
loves the way **Ian** reads her
favorite book.

The Farm

"Once upon a time, there was a farm.
And on that farm there was:

one tiny brown mouse,

squeak

two fluffy white lambs,

baa

baa

three sleepy little kittens,

meow

meow

meow

and four
very noisy
ducks . . .

"QUACK!
Quack!
Quack!

Quack!"
"Good reading, Ian!"

Little Neighbors
6
at number 6
More Driving with the Bugs
Here are the Bugs again, out driving in their backyard.
DIE
TRA
Milk
The Triplets like driving their milk truck.
1, 2, 3, Oops!
Keith likes driving his diesel train.
I ♥ Tractors
Mr. Thornton-Jones likes giving his friends a ride in his bus.
Jo-Jo likes driving her tractor. She painted the flowers herself.
Bob
Bob likes driving his scooter.

Stacie likes driving the Classy Lady.

Pauline and the girls like driving their steam train.

Tate likes driving his garbage truck. It is full of mud and stuff.

Giorgio likes driving his bulldozer.

Clemence likes driving his ambulance.

But most of all the Bugs love to . . .

bump and bash!
Beep!
Beep!
"Whee! I'm flying!"
Bob
"again, again!"
"Oops! my tea!"
Milk
DIES
TRA
1, 2, 3, Oops!
I ♥ Tractors
"Go, Jo-Jo, go!"
"Hey! Get off my roof!"
Hoot! Hoot!
"Oops! My glasses!"
"again, again!"

Bump!
"Gotcha, Keith!"
Bash!
Classy Lady
"Whee! This is fun!"
"OK, girls. Let's fly!"
STEAM TRAIN
"Gotcha, Tate!"
Bash!
Splash!
Mud and Stuff
TRASH 1
"Oops! My mud and stuff!"
Splash!
Beep!
"Yippee!"

# Painting with Ian

**Ian** really likes painting, and he is very good at it. Here he is getting all his paints ready. **Ian's** little sister, *Baby Jade*, is going to watch **Ian** paint. *Baby Jade* likes lots of colors, but **black** is her favorite.

"A blob of red and
a touch of green,"
says **Ian**.

"Now a dab of yellow
and a smidgen
of blue.
And finally . . .

"lots and lots of
Black!"
"Good
painting,
Ian!"

Little Neighbors at number 7

# More Making Things with Philip

Here's Philip again, making something else.

Now he needs:

1 cardboard box
2 broom handles
2 pieces of cardboard cut into shapes like this:

some tape

"Tape this here and this here," says Philip.

"Then step inside and . . .
Row, row, row your boat
Gently down the stream.
Merrily, merrily,
merrily, merrily,
Life is but a dream."

# more Messy Play with Kelly

Kelly is getting out all her bits and pieces in the living room. She is going to make **Ian** a card. Here comes Dad, who wants to help keep things neat.

"Let's put all your bits and pieces
and sticking things on your table,
and let's put some newspaper
on the floor."

"Put your apron on, Kelly, dear,"
says Dad.

"That's nice and neat,
darling. Now, I'm just
going to let the cat in.
Back in
a minute. . . ."

Ian

"Oh, Kelly, dear!"

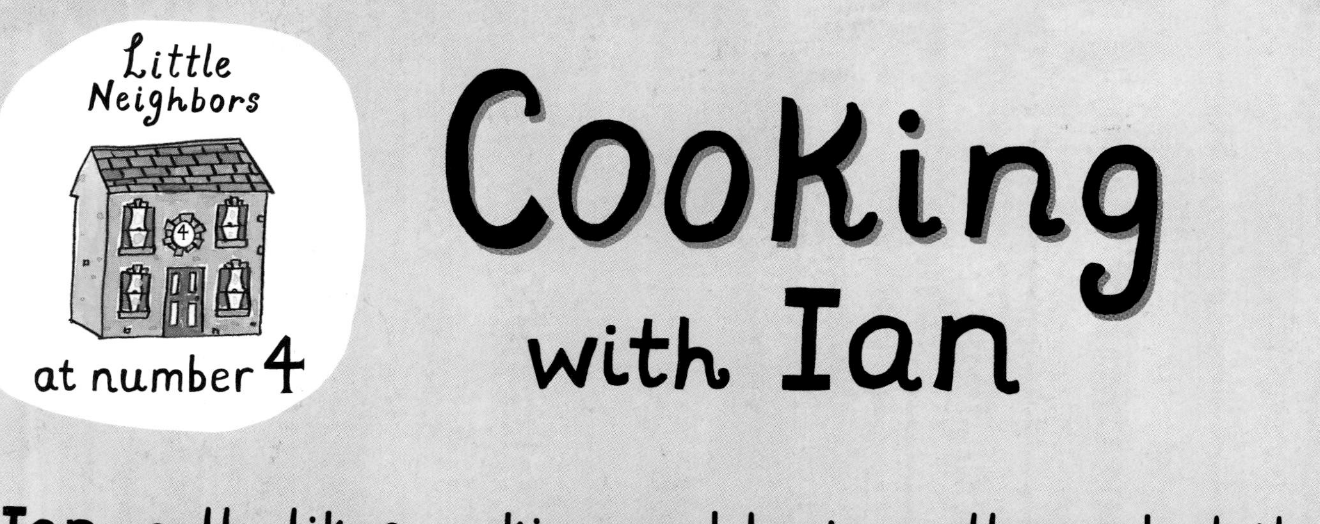


# Cooking with Ian

**Ian** really likes cooking, and he is really good at it. Here he is, getting out all the ingredients to make a cake. **Ian's** little sister, *Baby Jade*, loves the way **Ian** cooks.

"A little bit of
sugar and
some flour.
"Then crack some eggs,
add a pinch of salt
and one cup of milk.
Now give the whole
thing a really good . . .

"Whisk!"
"Good cooking, Ian!"

# Party Time!

All the *Little Neighbors* are in **Ian's** yard for a party. **Ian** really likes parties, and he is very good at them. He has put up lots of colorful balloons, made some delicious food, and here he is, putting on some party music.

We ♥ Parties
4

"Yeehaw!"
"Great party, Ian!"

# Sleeping

It has been a very busy day on Sunnyside Street.
But now it's time for sleeping.

Night-night, Tate.

Night-night, Keith.

Night-night, Triplets.

Night-night, Stacie.

Night-night,
Pauline and the girls.
Night-night,
Clemence.
Night-night, Jo-Jo.
Night-night, Mr. Thornton-Jones
and friends.
Night-night, Giorgio.
Night-night, Bob.

Night-night,
Kelly.

Night-night,
Philip.
tape /
pens / pencils

Night-night,
Ian.

Night-night,

Baby Jade.

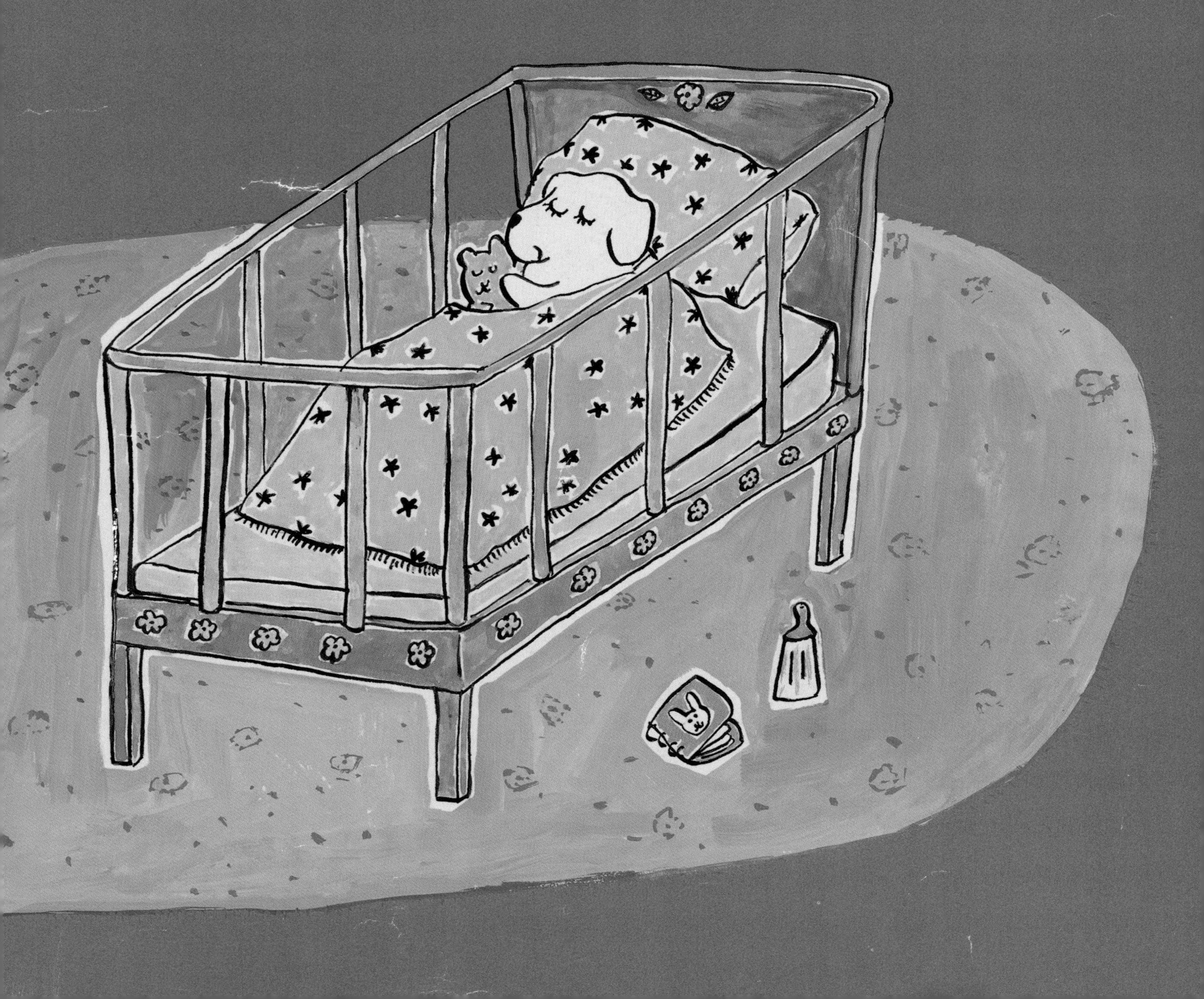

08 07
4
5